Want a free Ebook? Join my mailing list to get my monthly newsletter!

in praise of OLDER MEN

THE BOSTON SILVER FOXES

MATILDA MARTEL WRITING AS

MIA BARRETT

1. ZELDA

"Do you know what you need, little sister? You need a distraction. A wild one. And I think I know what that is." My sister, Zara, mumbles while she perfects the lines on her fire-engine red lip gloss. She's worked on it for the last fifteen minutes and I'm so bored, I've watched every second. She calls it her new signature color. No more pink for her.

"I don't need a distraction. I want to be alone." I grumble into my pillow, too exhausted to cry. The well's run dry. Ever since he changed his status from *Engaged* to *It's Complicated* to *Dating* in the span of seventy-two hours, crying feels foolish.

"Yes, a distraction. You need to sample the experienced hands of an older man. Doesn't that sound divine? I promise you. Those men know what they're doing. He'll mold your body like clay. He'll knead every curve, caress every valley until he shapes your supple teenage figure into his personal work of art. And when he's done, you'll beg him to do it again and again until you lose your voice from the multitude of chaotic orgasms that heavenly man wrenches from your tight virginal body, oh my God..." She trails off and gazes into the distance haunted by a memory she's never shared.

I emerge from my self-made cocoon, creep to the edge of the bed, and demand the rest of the story. "When the hell was this?!"

She shakes off the dazed look in her eyes and bats off my curiosity with a wave of her hand. "Never mind me. We're talking about you. It's high time you stopped auditioning for the convent and get laid. There are cocks on every street in Boston. Find a good one and hop on."

I ignore her entirely and continue with my inquisition.

"I thought you lost your virginity to Colin Butler?" I sit up, scramble to my feet, and reach for the fresh cookies she placed on my nightstand thirty minutes ago.

She shrugs. "Drop it, Zelda. It's a painful topic."

"No! Oh, my goodness. You didn't! For heaven's sake, did you lose your virginity to Conall Butler? He's practically Daddy's age!" My knees give out and I fall to the floor. I shove another cookie through my gaping mouth and try like hell to keep from giggling. Colin is movie-star handsome but Conall might be the beefiest beefcake that ever strutted his hot Irish ass down Louisburg Square.

I'm in awe of my sister's skills.

"When? Where? How the hell did it happen? Isn't he a lector a St. Joseph's? I'm sure he's in the Knights of Columbus. Is that all fake? Oh my God, Zara, spill it. I'm heartbroken and I need stories." I crawl towards her, salivating for more information.

This is huge. I can't believe she saw Conall Butler naked.

She tries to escape, but I reach for her ankle and hold on to her leg. "Come on. I'm not laughing at your pain. I just want details. That man's been a widower for ages. Every single woman in New England, and a few married ones, would sell their mother for a shot with Conall. When and how did you hook up?"

She wiggles me off her leg and makes a beeline into my closet. I follow with ears perked, desperate to hear every salacious word she utters.

"We hooked up. He made the first move. It was one time only. That's all I'll share for now. You don't get details until you have juicy tidbits of your own. You're twenty-one years old and you have nothing to share. Zip. Nada. Niente. Hook up with someone. Collect a juicy story and we'll compare notes. That's my deal." She taps my forehead and pushes me away.

"Fine. Keep your slut stories to yourself. You may go now. You suck at cheering me up." I stagger back into my bedroom and slump onto my bed.

She climbs onto the mattress next to me. "I meant what I said. You need a distraction. And men make the perfect distractions. One evening with a well-hung man, no strings, and you'll wake up with the best kind of amnesia. You'll forget all about Ethan and wonder what you ever saw in that steaming pile of excrement." She crosses her heart and throws away the key.

"Get dressed, doll face. Come out with me and the girls. We're headed to Monty's. That place is packed with college professors." She sprays my new perfume into the air and jumps into the mist. "You don't want to miss out."

I cover my face with my hands. "Stop talking. Oh, God! Please, stop talking. Stop trying to cheer me up. I don't want to feel better. I just want to disappear until my shame blows over."

Zara bounces on the mattress and shakes me. "Shame? Screw shame! Ethan's a whore, Zelda. He wanted your trust fund. I know it hurts, but you don't want a whore. That's gross." She wrinkles her nose and brings her forehead to mine. "Say it with me. We don't marry whores."

I grab my discarded hanky and nod through sniffles. "No whores."

"Would you like to know the best part?" She holds my hands in hers.

I look on, confused and agitated. There is no best part. My heart's in tatters. Mom, Aunt Cheryl, and Aunt Vivian are parked five houses away, surrounded by coffee and cake, calling the two hundred people who RSVP'd to my wedding to apologize for the last-minute cancellation. Ethan, my former fiancé, the man who I believed loved me, hasn't called or texted in three days. As soon as Daddy threatened to disinherit me, he dumped me so fast, he gave me whiplash.

He didn't state the obvious. He said he wasn't the marrying kind, after all. Then he blamed me. I'm too young to make a good wife. Too inexperienced. My sexual naiveté made him fall in love with someone else. There were a few more excuses, but I stopped listening when my world came crashing down around me.

He demanded his ring, then left me standing in the rain, crying and frozen in place. I don't remember the best part. Only utter humiliation. If Daddy hadn't wandered by and carried me inside, I might have been out there for hours.

"Zelda! Don't you get it? You get a do-over! You get to live and learn and love. This time you'll make better choices. Maybe you'll have some adventures and meet a man who worships you. You can meet the love of your life. The possibilities are endless, little sister. Now, get your ass in that shower and wash that horrible man out of your hair. Your big sister is taking you out on adventure number one." She tugs me out of bed and swings me towards the bathroom.

"No, Zara." I make a run for it, but she catches my arm and flings me forward, pushing me through onto the tiled floor.

"Sweetie, it's for your own good. Trust me." She flips on the shower, and hands me a razor. "Use this everywhere. You'll thank me later."

2. CARLO

hardly process the information. I don't think I've ever been called a whore. My assistant, June, reads the message again, but I make a slashing motion with my hand and beg her to stop. It's too brutal to stomach so soon after lunch.

"You have it coming." She folds the message neatly into four quarters and shoves it in her pocket.

"Destroy it. And never mention her name to me again." I bark my command, hoping my stern face and sharply pointed index finger make my point.

She blows the hair out of her face, then waves her hand to dismiss me. "Shut up, tough guy. I took the message on my personal notepad five minutes before I clocked back into work. Therefore, I own it. If I want to tell everyone in this office that Grace Sheridan dumped you like stinky trash, I will."

My eyes flare. The offense is too great to go unanswered. "She didn't dump me. We were never together. She just beat me to the punch." I jump forward to snatch it out of her hands, but she hops out of the way and slides towards the door.

"I'll hold my tongue if you do me a favor. I'll tear this

message. No, I'll shred it if you go to happy hour with me. I need a chaperone." She brings her hands to her hips and although her expression remains defiant, I detect a hint of desperation. *Bingo.*

"I'll get back to you." I offer a smirk and close my door.

"What?" Her jaw hits the floor. Her eyes bug. The last thing I see before she disappears behind the door is her small hand waving the message like a white flag.

I'll let her stew for an hour.

She thought she had me. She thought she could manipulate me into her web, but I don't appreciate dishonesty. If she wants a wingman, she can ask. June does excellent work. It's the only reason I've never fired her insubordinate ass. If she wants my help cruising the bars for her latest conquest, I'm more than happy to offer my assistance. But I won't be held hostage by Grace's message. *Or my ego.* Whatever this is.

I know where this is headed. *Chaperone, my ass.* What kind of twenty-eight-year-old woman needs a chaperone? She wants to go to Monty's.

Susan, my head of social media, and the person who keeps on top of everyone's life whether she wants to or not, told me June's got her eye on a hot new professor at MIT. According to Sue, he's a Physics genius with no social skills and an unhealthy love for bird watching.

That explains all of June's recent comments on Goldfinches and Blue Jays. She didn't even work them into the conversation. She just shouted out details on our walks to lunch. I mean, I appreciate all the work and dedication that goes into a hard-won seduction, but a little context never hurts.

I tap a few keys and refresh my mailbox. A new email appears. It's from June. I laugh to myself and click it open. It's an invitation request for a happy hour at Monty's. The time's set for 5:15. I propose 5:30, mark it as tentative, then hit send. I couldn't care less either way, but I enjoy giving her a hard time. Grace's rude message left me in a foul mood.

I'm not sure you can break up with someone if you're not technically involved in a committed relationship. And I don't do commitment.

She wants to make me out to be a villain, but she always knew we had no future. I laid out the parameters of our friendship from day one. We set boundaries. I checked in multiple times to make sure things were not getting out of hand, and I never lied about wanting exclusivity.

I'm not one of those men who lie to women to get what they want. I have nothing in common with those cads. Those gigolos are cut from a different cloth. No scruples. No heart or loyalty to anyone. They don't deserve the company of women.

They get what they want by tearing women down and making them question their confidence and sanity. They make thoughtless comments followed by daily jabs and then gaslight them into believing they're overly emotional and hard to handle. Women tolerate their philandering because they've tricked them into believing it's all in their head.

They're the worst kind of men. They're the men who hate women.

What kind of sick fuck hates women? Women are beautiful. They're magnificent. Resplendent. They're the irreplaceable sweetness that makes life worth living. All shapes. All sizes. I enjoy them so much, I can't limit myself to one.

But I'm no liar, and I'm certainly not a philandering gigolo. I believe in mutually beneficial transactional relationships. We get what we want for as long as we want, and then we move on to uncultivated pastures.

And I am always honest with the women I date.

If I get a bad feeling, if I detect heavy emotions could be on the line, I walk away before things get out of hand. When you've been around the block as much as me, you develop a sixth sense. The last thing I want to do is lead someone on. Only a prick would allow a woman to fall in love with him when he's got no intention of seeing it through.

I'm no saint, but I try damn hard not to be a prick.

"Carlo, we gotta be there by 5:15. If I don't arrive before him, he'll think I'm a stalker." June squeezes her giant head through a crack in my door and scares the hell out of me.

I shake my head and tap my watch. "It's nearly 5:00 now. We'll never make it." I power down my computer and reach for my bag. She's such a pain in the ass, but I'm dying to get a look at this guy. Susan gives him four stars and only deducts one because she thinks he's too old.

What's too old? I'm forty. If this guy's younger than me, I'm demoting her.

"Move it, Novello. My future babies are counting on you." She claps her hands and clears a path into the hall.

I scoff as we elbow one another on our way to the elevator. "That's what you said about your college sweetheart when he took you to lunch two months ago. If I recall, you came back early and swore off men forever."

"Don't remind me. Just move those old legs before he gets away."

"Stop calling me old. I'm in my prime. How old is your professor?" I tap the button and wait for the doors to close.

She ties her scarf and fluffs her hair as the car descends to the lobby. "Your age. He just turned forty. But he's a young forty. He doesn't have your kind of mileage."

I suck in a breath, appalled by the obvious implication but requiring further clarification. "What the hell does that mean?"

She leads the way through the lobby, eager to beat the rush of commuters streaming onto the sidewalk outside. "Don't play dumb. You know exactly what it means. Women like to play with you, but no one takes you seriously. I'm surprised Grace wanted more. You're like the futon we keep in our apartments in college. We'll get great use out of you. For a while, we might even think we love you. But no one's taking you to the big house with a mortgage. Futons are gross. Too much wear and tear. All our friends slept on it. By the time they get to a certain age, it's time to take them to the junkyard or set them on fire."

"Are you trying to piss me off?" I open the door to Monty's and wait for her hateful ass to walk in. "I think I'd rather be called a whore than a futon."

She laughs to herself. "That's fine by me."

3. ZELDA

"THIS PLACE LOOKS LIKE A LIBRARY!" MY MOOD INSTANTLY brightens when we step through a heavy oak door complete with stained glass panels. It's not a typical watering hole or club like I expected.

Everything from the bar to the chairs looks weathered or antique. Bookcases with actual books, not knickknacks, line one wall. Photos of old Boston, not neon signs line the other. The crowd is older than us. The room's packed with professionals eager to blow off steam after a long day at work. No one appears to be shitfaced at 4:30 in the afternoon.

This is a long way from the average college pub Zara frequents.

"You'll love it. It's so much easier to hear yourself think and carry a conversation. Plus, the men are men, little sister. No boys allowed." Zara wiggles her eyebrows and giggles. She places one foot in front of the other, her trick to make her hips sway like an old Hollywood siren, and leads us through a small group of well-dressed men on our way to the bar.

I clutch my purse to my chest to shield my cleavage and cluelessly follow. With every step, the reclaimed wood floor squeaks under the ridiculous slingback pumps Zara wrestled onto my feet. They're not practical for a cool Autumn day, but the only ones delicate enough to wear with this dress. I wish I'd brought a wrap or cardigan. It's meant for warmer weather and far more revealing than anything I typically wear. Zara insisted, and once she gets something in her head, it's hard to talk her down.

One by one, we take our place at the bar like three single girls out on the town. Just me, Zara and my best friend, Evie. Zara's friends backed out at the last minute. We're letting our hair down and moving on to greener pastures. Footloose and fancy free without a care in the world. That's the mantra for the evening. If I repeat it a few more times, maybe it'll sink in.

"We'll have three whiskeys. Nothing too expensive. Jack Daniels is fine. Two fingers." Zara orders for us.

"I'll need to see some identification." The bartender eyeballs Evie and me. We're not regulars, and since we only turned twenty-one over the summer, his scrutiny is justified.

We fumble through our purses, crack open our wallets, and quickly slide over our driver's licenses one at a time. When he hands mine back, I lean in and alter my drink order. "Whiskey straight sounds too strong for my blood. Can you make mine a whiskey sour?"

"What?!" Zara voices her disappointment loud and clear. I don't care. I'm not drinking ethanol just to please her.

"Oh, me too. Whiskey sour sounds yummy." Evie chimes in as she shoves her I.D. into her *Hello Kitty* wallet. Thrilled to be free from her aunt's watchful gaze, she paddles her heels on the footrest and yips when her phone vibrates on her fingers.

"What's wrong?" I sneak a peek into her purse.

She stares at her message then pushes her phone deep into her bag, ignoring the third text she's received in the last thirty minutes. "It's nothing. Daddy's being weird."

Evie didn't grow up in Boston like Zara and me. She's from a sleepy hamlet thirty minutes from here, where everyone knows everyone, and one family runs the show. She dragged me there last year for her father's fiftieth birthday party, and I'm not sure I ever want to go again. It's not normal. It's full of country club playboys and Stepford wives. I don't blame Evie for wanting to break away.

"Let's make a toast." Zara calls our attention back to her and the bartender serving our whiskies. I take a quick sip, just in case I need to request an additional splash of sour mix, then give the guy my thumbs up.

Evie holds her arm high and clears her throat. "I'd like to make one too. Thank you for inviting me. I needed this." She kicks back half her drink before Zara stops her.

"That's not a toast, Eve. That's a thank you. Save some drink for the toast. It's bad luck." She clears her throat, smiles, then lifts her whiskey. "This is to my baby sis, Zelda. She dodged a huge bullet this week. But greater things are on the horizon. I've talked to Dad, and he's altered your travel arrangements for next week. Instead of cancelling everything, you and I leave for Mexico on Monday!" She jumps off her barstool and bounces for joy.

My mouth falls open. *My honeymoon?* They've turned my honeymoon into a girls' trip? Evie's shaky hand falls on my shoulder in a silent show of support. She knows my sister means well, but she also knows Ethan chose Cozumel. I wanted Paris. Sandy beaches and piña coladas aren't my idea of a good time. Last time I tried, I fried my skin the first day and spent the next three under an umbrella reading trashy novels. I can do that at home.

Zara senses my dismay and ends her happy dance. "Aren't you excited?"

Evie cuts in. "How was that a toast? That was clearly more of a travel announcement."

I climb down from my seat and shimmy my skirt into place. My sister's wide blue eyes flicker with waves of regret, fearing she's driven me deeper into mourning. Zara's not a selfish person. She wouldn't plan this trip to romp around the Mexican Riviera and work on her tan. It's not in her nature.

I close my eyes, take a deep breath, and unclench my teeth. "When do we leave?"

Her misty eyes flare open, and she throws her arms around my neck. "We're going to have so much fun! Screw that bastard! I can't wait to post photos of you in your bikini all over social media. He'll die when he realizes what he missed out on." She licks her finger, touches my behind and makes a sizzling sound. I'm not sure if I giggle out of obligation or because it's too corny for words.

"Evie, watch my drink. I need to go to the bathroom and throw some water on my smoking hot ass before this place catches fire." I pull down my skirt, pull my hair forward to hide my boobs, and try my best to strut confidently to the ladies' room. My heels wobble on the uneven floor. A few salacious cat calls throw me off my trajectory, but I push through and channel Marilyn Monroe, Beyoncé, and Aunt Viv, who's got one hell of a sashay.

She told me the women in our family have a long history of man-eating. Nana was the Belle of Boston in her day. She played grandpa like a Stradivarius violin until he was so distraught, he threatened to become a priest if she didn't accept his proposal. I'm not sure how that sweetened the pot, but all's well that ends well. They just celebrated fifty-five years of wedded bliss. I can only hope to aspire to such greatness.

Zara's right. Screw Ethan. The hell with him. *Good riddance.*

As I round the corner, I square my shoulders, toss my dark locks into the wind and thrust my proud breasts forward. With my head held high and my mind reeling with thoughts of revenge, I slam my adventurous boobs straight into the chest of an unsuspecting gentleman exiting the men's room.

"Oh, my God!" I push away, humiliated and terrified that I've accosted a complete stranger with my tits. In the chaos, I snag my mother's heirloom bracelet on his waistcoat button and fight like crazy to tear it loose. When I tug back, I pull him towards me, smothering him once again and feeling my face catch fire as he gently squeezes my palm to calm me down.

Dear lord, strike me dead where I stand.

"Miss, stand still. Let me get it." His rugged hands slacken their grip and I watch with wide eyes as he gently unwinds the delicate chain from his vest button.

Inches apart, his heavenly scent floats into my face and I sneak a peek through my disheveled bangs. My heart skips a beat. My tummy roils. He's too lovely for words.

"There! You're free!" His deep silvery voice elicits a girlish giggle. When he lifts his dark gaze and curves his plump lips into a wicked smile, I nearly swoon.

"Thank you... sir." I spin on my heels, almost lose my balance, then flee.

This is too much too soon. I thought I was ready to explore my bad girl side. Hate and half a whiskey sour made me crazy with vengeance, but raunchy Zelda won't emerge tonight. Liquor fuels bad decisions and getting dumped makes them worse.

I've made up my mind. For now, I must suppress my wickedness for the greater good.

I wash my hands and make the sign of the cross.

Were his eyes brown or hazel?

4. CARLO

"Carlo?" My head snaps to attention, but I ignore the voice. A pair of shapely legs and the voluptuous curves of a dark-haired angel sidle pass my table on their way back to the bar. My heart skips a beat. Then another. It's the damnedest thing.

My mouth slacks as I gaze transfixed at the most sumptuous pair of breasts my hungry eyes have ever seen. The thin fabric of her dress leaves little to my imagination. They're flawless. Supple, smooth, perfectly round and almost too much for my hands. But something tells me I could manage.

Where the hell have they been all my life?

Treading lightly in her black stiletto pumps, she approaches her friends and discreetly peeks over her shoulder. Her frightened gaze meets mine for no more than a second, and her mossy green eyes grow obscenely wide.

Luscious pink lips part with surprise and quiver once. Just once. And my mouth waters to taste them. Every hair stands on end. Heat curls inside me. My pulse races and my cock thickens against my thigh. No one's ever aroused me with such little provocation.

"Who are you staring at?" A slap to the back of my head startles me out of my lusty daydream, and I blink twice to refocus on June's peevish expression.

My clogged throat can hardly make out words. I wipe the drool gathering at the corners of my mouth and reach for my drink. Stammering like an idiot, I point to the group of women gathered at the bar. "The girl in the black dress. The one in the middle. Tell me you know who that is."

"I don't." She smacks on a handful of peanuts, annoyed that her professor has yet to arrive.

"She knows. Everyone knows." Susan, who refused to be denied a front-row seat to June's hunting expedition, corrects her lies. "That's Zelda Haverty. Arthur Haverty's daughter. Tomorrow should be her wedding day. *The social event of the season*." She uses rabbit ears to crush my world.

"Wait, a minute... *should* be?" That word almost escaped me.

Before she continues, she slurps her drink and tosses a handful of miniature pretzels in her mouth. "The groom dumped her three days ago. It's all Boston high society can talk about. It's bad enough getting caught up with a man like Ethan Wells. Imagine the humiliation of being dumped right before your wedding."

My heart aches for her, but that emotion quickly passes. In what universe does a goddess so divine marry a man like Ethan Wells? But she didn't marry him. That scoundrel deemed this heavenly woman unworthy of his fidelity and affection. Is he out of his mind? Of course he is. He's vile. That's why I didn't hire his unworthy ass when his cousin, sitting next to me, asked me for a favor.

I cast a stern glare at the dishwater blonde to my right. "What do you have to say for yourself?"

June gazes straight ahead and ignores my scowl. "Don't give me those eyes, Novello. Ethan sucks. I can't help it if we're related. My aunt asked for a favor and I gave you fair warning before the interview. When you passed on him, I never gave you grief and you know it." She scans the room for her professor, worried she'll miss her chance, then returns to the conversation. "Anyway, quit eyeballing Zelda with your *dirty old man* eyes. She's a nice girl. And she's nursing a broken heart. The last thing she needs is a roll in the hay with the Italian Stallion of Beacon Hill."

"Leave him alone. I think Carlo's exactly what she needs. No strings. No fuss or drama. He's a perfect afternoon snack to clean the pipes and send her on her merry way. After him, she'll move on with a whole new attitude on life." Susan offers a backhanded compliment that makes me feel like I need a shower.

June shakes her head and wields her straw with authority, lecturing the table like she knows all about life, sex and snagging the perfect man. "I don't know, Sue. According to my Aunt Ash, Ethan's mother, Zelda's a good girl. A very good girl, if you know what I mean. Too good for her son."

She tilts her head and drops her voice to a whisper. "Apparently, Ethan liked his women with more experience. If you get my drift." She rolls her hand like an ocean wave and clicks her tongue.

I scoff, then shift my gaze to Zelda. They may be right. She looks innocent. While she nurses her drink and makes small talk with her friend, she shimmies into her bar stool and fidgets with her skirt. It's not that short, but she seems preoccupied with exposing too much thigh every time she tries to cross her legs. When she tries again, my hungry eyes glimpse a flash of her right inner thigh and I nearly fall out of my chair.

She knows I'm watching her. There's no way she can't feel the weight of my depraved leering from fifteen feet away. But she refuses to engage. She clasps her hands and stares nervously from side to side, avoiding my gaze at all costs. All I need is a crumb of encouragement. One smile. A dreamy gaze. A few flirtatious sweeps of those long dark lashes and I'll be all over her like a cheap suit.

"Hey, did you hear me?" June nudges my elbow. "Stop gawking. You're too old and too twisted for Zelda Haverty. Men like you don't get to play with naïve college girls looking for husbands. Do this poor girl a favor and stick to your divorcees and party girls."

My mouth parts then snaps back in place. I grumble a sarcastic reply under my breath, then drown it with my drink. She's a broken record, but for some strange reason, her words sting. I could say something rude. There is no shortage of insults to fling regarding her non-existent love life, but I hold my tongue and skip the tantrum. Without thinking, my gaze helplessly returns to the angel seated at the bar. The raucous noise buzzing over our head drops to a whisper and the only sound I hear is the gentle hum of Zelda's honeyed voice.

If I was alone, nothing would stop me from approaching such a beautiful woman. Perhaps she's vulnerable. I'd never take advantage of a woman nursing a broken heart. I'm a man of conviction who doesn't need to sleep with every woman he meets.

This could be an exercise in self-control. After all, she needs to know not all men are Ethans. There are men who would move mountains to claim the woman they love. I may not be one of them, but we're out there by the thousands just waiting for a beautiful doll like her.

"Look at him. He's salivating like a bloodhound." June whispers to Susan, annoying me further and making me more determined than ever to shake them loose.

"Hey, those guys look like professors. Is your bird lover in that group?" I point to the door and immediately alter the mood at the table.

While Susan scopes out the sizable crowd of men, June runs her hands through her hair. She retrieves a tiny compact from her purse and checks her lips. June's a pretty girl, but she tries way too hard. The only thing she needs to work on is her expectations.

"Oh, my God. He's here." Susan spots him first and hands June her pocket perfume. "One spritz on your wrist, then dab on the other. It works with your pheromones."

June does as instructed, then turns to me. "How do I look? Don't be mean."

My eyes narrow as I inspect her work from top to bottom. "You look like a tramp."

"Good, that's the look I want." She breathes a sigh of relief. "We're going to mingle with the hot professors now. You may leave, or you can make your move. I have little doubt which one you'll choose."

She smooths down her skirt and loops her purse over her shoulder. "Promise me you won't be a dick. She's a good girl. Some people aren't capable of meaningless sex. No matter what they say, they're just not wired that way."

I nod in agreement. She's right. There's something about this girl that sets off all the right buttons. And I can't be trusted.

As they walk away, I watch a tall man emerge from the crowd and make a beeline for Zelda's small party. I blink and refocus to get a better look through the band of suits blocking my view. It's my neighbor and client, Conall Butler. I know him well. He's slightly older and if I remember from the last time I spotted him at the gym, in slightly better shape. I can hardly fault him for that. He's notoriously celibate. If I hadn't been with a woman in years, I'd probably spend every spare minute burning off excess energy at the gym too.

I hope he hasn't decided to break his streak on my Zelda. *My Zelda?* I shake the thought out of my head and watch him approach the trio at the bar. No, it's a duo. One girl has flown the coop.

Fortunately, Zelda isn't his target. He homes in on the girl to her left and demands she speak to him. He looks rumpled and sweaty, like he jogged here in his work clothes. Stunned by his presence, she pushes him away and flees like a frightened cat.

Oh, no, Zelda's alone. *That's a damn shame.*

5. ZELDA

 He hands the miniature drink menus to our bubbly waitress, who tripped over herself to serve us. She thrills when his masculine hands brush against her fingers. The blush on her cheeks spreads to her ears, then covers her neck. She fumbles for her pen and scribbles furiously while her eyes drift up and down, cataloging every inch of Carlo Novello's powerful physique. I can't blame her for gawking. Ten seconds in his presence and your eyes have a mind of their own.

If I wasn't presently furious at every man on earth, I might be drawn into those heavenly hazel eyes. I'm almost positive I'd float towards those amazing man lips like a moth to a flame. But I'm off men. For now, anyway. *Not forever.* I'd eventually like a family and although they're horrible creatures, they come in handy when you want children.

Until I figure out where I'm going. Until I learn the secrets of my heart, men have no power over me. They stink. *They all stink.*

And yet, this one smells rather nice. *Is that cedar? Bergamot?* It can't be his natural scent. Nature wouldn't be so cruel. She wouldn't kneecap women everywhere by giving him that kind of power.

Well, whatever it is, it's divine.

"Tell me the truth, Zelda. What did you see in Ethan Wells? I interviewed him last year and he must have been on his best behavior if he wanted a job with my company. And yet, I couldn't stand more than fifteen minutes in his presence. How in the world did that Neanderthal talk you into marriage?" He slides my drink across the table and tilts his head to examine me closer. When his smoldering gaze meets mine, I pat my tummy, soothing the horde of butterflies that mysteriously appeared when he invited me to sit at his table.

"Are you calling me gullible?" I bring the glass to my lips and try to disguise the nervous shiver in my voice. With every passing minute, my heart sinks under the weight of clarity. A stranger told me what I already know in my heart to be true. I didn't need it said with such glaring honesty, but at least he's not treating me like a wounded animal. I've had enough pity to last a lifetime.

To my surprise, he nods. "You must be if you almost married Ethan. Why don't you know your worth, sweetheart? You're a feast on the eyes. Every man in this room would kill to take you home tonight."

My eyes fly open. I turn to peek over my shoulder and spot a crowd of gentleman eye me with salacious intent. I grip my grandmother's pearls tightly in my fingers and feel the throbbing rhythm of my racing heart. *This is ludicrous.* Why am I entertaining this kind of talk with a strange man? I'm not this kind of girl. I don't care what Zara says. These types of adventures aren't helpful in my situation. They only make things worse.

"I don't want to talk about Ethan. He's in my past and it isn't healthy to dwell on the past. I met him when I was younger. My expectations were much lower, and I let him con me into accepting less than I deserved. I'm just glad I don't have to spend the next few miserable years figuring out what I know now." I exhale with relief and think about the words that tumbled out of my mouth. They've been on the tip of my tongue for days but wallowing in self-pity took too much time to piece them together.

He quirks an eyebrow, smiles, then lifts his glass in a toast. "Fuck Ethan. May he rot in whatever hell he creates for himself."

I hold back. "Oh, no. I don't want to toast to his misfortune."

"Zelda..." His voice grates as he lifts his hand to his throat and loosens his tie. "He doesn't deserve your kindness. He humiliated you and never hid his infidelities or his motives for marrying into your family. Lift your goddamn glass now and toast that he might die a fiery death of his own making."

We clink and slam the rest of our drinks in one swig.

The second he sets his empty tumbler on the table, the waitress abandons her other guests, pushes past her co-workers and flings herself towards his glass.

"Can I get you another whiskey? And another Cape Cod?" Out of breath, she offers her best *come hither* look and pushes her breasts into his face.

"And a club soda, please." I interject.

"Yes, and the tab." He doesn't need to do much to encourage her flirtation. His body language is a testament to his nature. Mr. Carlo Novello looks like he's made specifically for female amusement. He's a naughty girl's Disneyland. Every ride is an E-ticket, and the park is open twenty-four hours. When he hands her a black American Express, she scurries away, overcome with emotion.

I squint and purse my lips. Zara briefed me before her hasty abandonment. Carlo's notorious. "It must feel nice to have so many women fawn over you. Is that why you never married?" I sip what's left of my drink and pretend to be intrigued by something on the happy hour menu. There's a special on appetizers. Two for the price of one. I have no appetite to speak of, but concentrating on his long fluttering man lashes and the angle of his strong chin does not serve me well.

He tries not to smile. "I believe everyone should know and understand their own limitations. I fear mine would be fidelity. Philanderers enter committed relationships because they want their partner to be faithful to them and never intend to reciprocate. That's not my style. There's no sense in pretending I can limit myself to one woman. I don't think I'm built that way. And I prefer to be honest with the women I date. Anything else would be disrespectful."

His candor unsettles me. After my recent experience, it's hard not to appreciate his sincerity. "May I ask you a personal question?"

His perfect masculine lips twitch with curiosity. "You may ask. I can't promise I'll answer."

I nod and accept his terms. "How do you do it?"

"Do what?" A line forms between his brow as he straightens his tie. He must assume I'm asking for specifics on his techniques. Why on earth would I care about those?

"How do you keep from falling in love? You appear to be a warm and caring individual. But you're not a young man. If you've spent the last twenty years having intimate relations with countless beautiful women, surely one or two got under your skin. Only a robot never falls in love." I fiddle with my pearls and make way for the waitress.

He opens his mouth, then freezes. His eyes narrow, then shift from left to right as he considers my words. "Are you implying I'm old?"

My eyes grow and stay wide as I stare at one of the most devastatingly handsome men I've ever met shrink into his seat with a sudden case of teenage girl insecurity. I never realized men were so sensitive about their age. If I were half as cruel as my sister, this could be fun.

I wag my head with a touch of frustration. Just enough to make him feel silly. "I'm not sure what part of my question inferred anything more than your experience. But if this is your way of avoiding the question, I understand. I sometimes forget falling in love is a privilege. Not everyone experiences it. I apologize if it's a painful subject for you."

He balks. "Now you're just being a pain in the ass."

"Not at all." I hold my tongue. I'm here because he gave me little choice. I was about to leave when he swept in like a whirlwind of testosterone and a chance for distraction.

A minute of awkward silence passes before he finally speaks. "You want to provoke me by calling me a fraud. Your stuffy sensibilities probably find my way of life offensive. I don't believe in delayed gratification. And you shouldn't either. Don't wait for what you want. If you want something. Make it happen. You patiently waited for love and life gave you Ethan Wells. You should be furious. The Ethans of the world live their lives to excess, then wait for Zeldas to clean up their mess. You're better than that. Don't wait for someone to complete you. Seek what you want and take it." He slams his fist on the table and I almost jump out of my seat.

I shake my head and huff, chafed by his oversimplified assessment of my stuffy sensibilities. "I did no such thing. You spoke plainly about your elaborate system of mindless, soulless sexual satisfaction and I'd just like to know how you pull it off." I ruffle my feathers. He doesn't know me well enough to accuse me of judging him, and he doesn't know everything about Ethan and me. I can cut loose if the mood strikes. I'm not some delicate flower incapable of enjoying the seedier side of life.

I don't care what Ethan says. I'm no goody-two-shoes. That was the old me. The idiot who believed in soul mates, true love, and all that dumb crap you read about in books.

I take a sip from my drink and clear my throat. "Perhaps, I'd like to familiarize myself with your methods. I'm a single woman now. I have no desire to jump from one serious relationship into another. There are wild oats that need sowing and a city of men just outside those doors that can make that happen." I point to the oak door leading out to the street and snap my fingers.

His brow creases. "I hate when bartenders are heavy-handed with women's drinks. He thinks he's doing the man a favor, but he doesn't anticipate girls like you. And he certainly doesn't expect men like me." He yanks the glass out of my hand and sniffs it. His eyes grow twice their size. His mouth twists with agitation. He slams the drink on the table and lifts his hand to call the waitress.

"Girls like me? Men like you?" I reach for my drink, but he holds it out of reach. Confused by his odd behavior, I reach for my purse and fumble for my phone. It was a mistake to keep company with a man like Carlo. Zara was wrong about older men. They're not hot. They treat you like little girls. And I'm no man's little girl.

Except for Daddy, but that's different.

"Girls who can't handle their liquor." He snaps. "You don't drink often. Do you? And don't bother lying. I can tell. It's one of my powers." His lips press into a thin line as he gives me the once over.

"You don't know what I do or don't do. I can't help it if the cranberry juice disguises the vodka. Stop talking to me like I work for you. Why am I still here? I'm leaving." I reach for my phone, but he holds his hand out to stop me.

"Forgive me. I'll explain, but first, let me take you to dinner. You've got big plans for sexual domination. *I get it.* But you've been compromised by liquor. I'll tell you my secrets while I sober you up with food." His eyes flicker with sincerity while his lips curve into a suspicious grin.

"Are you making fun of me?"

He nods and offers his hand. "Yes. But my invitation still stands. Let's go."

6. ZELDA

"Chatham? What do you mean you're going to Chatham?" Zara wipes the sleep from her eyes and shuffles to the fridge in search of orange juice. Smudges of last night's eyeliner dot her cheekbones as she pours herself a glass and quietly pads towards the coffeemaker.

She's not herself. As much as I want to give her hell for ditching me last night, the sister code prevents me from getting my due. Conall Butler appeared out of the ether and chased her into the night. At worst, she's in pain. At the very least, she's out of sorts.

Don't get me wrong. She's not off the hook. But I'm obligated to go easy.

"I thought we wanted to do a spa day." She reminds me of plans she made without my approval. I never wanted a spa day. Why would I want something reminiscent of a bridal day of beauty? The similarity escaped her when she made the reservations. I should have said something, but I didn't want to make waves. No more of that nonsense.

I shrug and continue to whisk my eggs. I planned to give her the news last night. When Carlo walked me home shortly after a lovely evening of dinner and inappropriate conversation, I stayed up as long as I could to spill precious details to my only sister. I think I heard her come home at 3:00, but I might have been dreaming.

"Are you ignoring me?" She circles past me, hovering too close to the stove and deliberately crowding my workspace.

"Stop that. You and Evie are on my shit list. You drag me to a bar against my will and better judgment. Then you leave me there all by my lonesome on the day before the day I was supposed to get married. I felt like an idiot." I pour my eggs into the frying pan and stir them harder than I should.

"You're getting egg everywhere." Zara takes over.

"You know I'm sorry. I hadn't spoken to Conall Butler in four years! The man's lost his mind. What happened with you? Did Carlo approach you? Why are you going to Marblehead? I thought we were getting ready for Monday and keeping your mind off the wedding." She pushes my scrambled eggs onto a plate and hands me a fork.

"That was too many questions at once." I take my plate and set it on the table. While I butter my toast, I try to remember which question came first.

"Fortunately, Carlo saved me from humiliation. We had a nice chat, then he invited me for dinner. He's the one who suggested a day trip out of Boston to get my mind off this wedding crap. Out of sight, out of mind. If I leave town, I won't see the church or run into guests giving me sad eyes. We put our heads together, searched online, and set our sights on Cape Cod. Chatham seemed nicest. We can see the foliage, shop for antiques, climb the lighthouse and I heard they have the best lobster rolls. He's picking me up in an hour." I shovel my eggs onto my bread and build a sandwich.

"Excuse me?" Zara's gaping mouth confuses me.

"What? Did you want some?" I offer her a bite, then remember my manners and cut off a piece with my knife.

"You're going antiquing with Carlo Novello? Zelda! He's a scoundrel. You don't see autumn leaves and drink hot apple cider with men like him. You drink martinis and have filthy one-night stands with them. He's supposed to be a distraction. Don't you know what a distraction means? You're doing this all wrong!" She plops her behind into the chair opposite from mine and sinks her face into her hands.

I glance at the clock on the stove and take a few more bites in quick succession. Mumbling and spitting crumbs, I try to explain. "We're friends. I'm not falling for him. He's hot, and he makes me laugh. Plus, he's helping me understand more about men. I'm clueless, Zara. *You know I am.* Ethan made an ass out of me. I won't let that happen again."

She wrings her hands with anxiety and scoots to the edge of her seat. "You'll get attached. He's charming with years of experience wooing women under his belt. I'm not sure you can help it."

My shoulders sink. I slide out of my chair and place my empty plate in the dishwasher. She's not overreacting. If the tables were turned, I'd be just as concerned.

"I have zero expectations. Less than zero. Carlo doesn't do relationships. And I want nothing to do with them for the foreseeable future. If I did, I wouldn't choose Carlo. He's too old for me. I've got the rest of this semester off before I return to school in the spring. That's two months to make up for lost time. Two months to do *what I want to do.*" I drink the rest of my juice and set the glass in the sink.

"And I called Dad this morning. We leave for Mexico on Wednesday. Not Monday. I don't want to feel rushed." I sprint upstairs before she has a chance to respond. In my wake, I hear a gasp, then the fast pace of footfalls gaining on me in the hall.

"Wednesday! But I'm ready to leave now." She screams as she

bangs on my bedroom door. "You don't understand. I need to get the hell out of Dodge, Zelda. Conall won't take no for an answer and I'm weak. If he finds out I'm still in town, he'll come by. And if he comes by, I'll break."

I unlock the door and stick my face through the crack. "Sorry, but it's done. Dad emailed us the new itineraries this morning. Hide out at Mom and Dad's until then. Carlo said I should grab life by the balls and that's what I'm doing. Hey, why don't you hang out with Evie? She's acting weird and swears her family's out to get her."

Zara's eyes widen. Her face contorts into a grimace. "Carlo? Who the hell is Carlo? Is he your sister? Is he your new best friend? Eve's family is out to get her. Dad says they're crazy." She barges in, then follows me into the bathroom.

While I run a bath, she kicks her feet, flails her arms in a deranged tantrum, then leans against the wall and sinks to the floor. "I don't think I like this new Zelda. She sounds like a jerk."

7. CARLO

There's more to Zelda than her beautiful face. And so much more than her hauntingly beautiful body. Although every inch of those delicious curves kept me up half the night with a desperate ache for release, my mind often drifted to parts I generally overlook. Self-preservation pleaded with me to cancel our adventure, but I couldn't bear to let her down.

Today, I help her forget. Zelda Haverty was born to be a goddess. If I can help build back her confidence after the world kicked her in the teeth, then I have an obligation to see this through. This isn't about me and my selfish desires to spend time with a beautiful woman. Not entirely, anyway.

I like her. She makes me laugh. It seems like a simple thing, but in my world, it's not. The women I meet are as tough as nails. They take what they want and save their softer side for the men who warm their beds. Zelda's not experienced enough to play those games. Her sweet nature warms my heart. It's no sacrifice to spend the day with her. It was my idea, and I've been looking forward to it since I dropped her off last night.

But at the moment, she's wearing on my nerves.

"I think we're lost, Carlo." She scrolls through her phone, lifts it up to the corner of the car's cabin, then shakes it. "I can't get a decent signal, but I swear I saw a sign that read we were headed towards Falmouth. That's the wrong way."

We don't have a signal. We lost it fifteen minutes ago when the clouds rolled in. My service is always spotty when I'm on the cape, but it's abysmal when it rains. It doesn't matter, anyway. I know my way to the coast. I've been here a hundred times. Not a hundred. Maybe a dozen. Work doesn't allow me to come as often as I'd like.

"We're supposed to pass Falmouth." I assure her with a cocky tone I can't disguise. Sensing her anxiety, I take a small liberty and pat her thigh to calm her nerves. The touch of her warm skin sends electric currents coursing through my veins and straight into my groin. My eyes flash back to the road. This is neither time nor place to entertain impure thoughts. We're having a friendly adventure, and this is an opportunity for growth.

Screw June. I'm more than a two-dimensional male sex doll. I can be a friend too.

Zelda unbuckles her seatbelt, tucks her leg under her ass and positions her body to face me. Bristling with anger, she taps her phone and draws my attention to her screen. "Hey, Magellan. Falmouth is down here. Chatham is way over here. If we want to get here." She taps to the east. "Then we don't need to drive due south."

Her nose wrinkles and her swollen cherry lips form a distinctive pout. My heart flutters like a teenage boy first discovering the wonder of girls. I'm overcome with an out-of-control desire to swerve to the side of the road, shift the car into park, haul her into my lap and kiss that pout clean off the face of the earth. Would she mind? Does she want my kiss? No, she's a vulnerable woman and I won't to take advantage of the situation.

"Well?" She snaps as she returns to her seated position and

fastens her seatbelt. "Are you going to tell me you've decided to take me to Falmouth to save face?"

"No, smartass. I'll make a turnaround up ahead." I laugh to myself and try to keep my eyes off her legs and strictly on the road. At the next service station, I flip my turn signal and make a U-turn back towards the main highway.

"Sorry, I yelled." Her bright green eyes find mine and the corners of my mouth twitch into a lazy smile. My heart buzzes to life with an unfamiliar flame that threatens to consume me in a fiery blaze. This is unprecedented. I'm sure it'll pass. It has no choice.

"No. I'm an idiot." She tried to warn me we were headed the wrong way and my fat head wouldn't listen. Women are such remarkable creatures. I don't know how they've tolerated men for so long.

"Do you think we should just turn back to Boston? By the time we get there, we'll only have an hour or two of sunlight. Seems like a waste." She reclines in her seat and I lose myself in the rich brown locks tumbling down her shoulders. My head dizzies. The tide approaches and my poor unsuspecting cock throbs against my leg.

"No! We press on Haverty. The day is young." My firm tone startles her gaze back to mine.

"But what will we do in the rain? Not much sightseeing after the sun goes down." She sucks in a deep breath and her mouthwatering breasts heave salaciously. This girl is unbelievable. Hoping to force myself flaccid, I think of my mother's knee surgery and breathe a sigh of relief when the tide recedes.

"The rain will probably let up soon, anyway."

"Do you think?" She stares bemused at the dark clouds ahead.

"The sun's just past those clouds. I'm sure of it." Nonsense tumbles freely from my lust-muddled brain. I don't want to give up our day. Not yet.

Thunder booms and lightning crashes a few miles ahead. Of course it does. What better way for God to spend a Saturday afternoon than making an ass out of Carlo Novello?

Zelda jumps closer. Her green eyes grow wide with fear and her hand claws my waist. "Maybe we should pull over. It's coming down harder."

I curl my arm around her shoulder and pull her closer. "We just have to get through these bands ahead. Barnstable isn't far. Let's stop there and wait it out." I don't know what I'm talking about. I'm a terrible driver. It's not often I drive myself anywhere. The further we travel, the more the water gathers on the road. We're alone. Smarter drivers have shunned the low-lying highway and moved to higher ground. But my stubborn ass presses on.

Her trembling arm winds around me, and she uses my body heat to soothe her fears. I breathe in the scent of her perfume and discreetly shift the cock tenting my trousers. There's no reason I should be this hard. She's a lovely girl with an incredible body, but I know tons of beautiful women. I can't focus. I'm going to kill us. My windshield wipers can't keep up with the heavy droplets obscuring my vision, and her breasts are close enough to lick. I'll go mad before I get my chance.

She spots a sign and gestures with her finger. "Over there. That sign says Barnstable in seven miles. That's not so far. Can we push through a bit longer?"

My mind spins. My resolve crumbles. Seven miles is an eternity. My sweaty hands grip the steering wheel as my eyes scan the road for shelter. Nothing appears. Nothing for miles. The rap of the rain on the hood of my car matches the jackhammering beat of my heart. I can hear it thumping loudly in my ears, mocking my weakness and swift descent.

"Are you okay?" Zelda wriggles back to her side. No doubt the lewd bulge in my trousers has given her second thoughts about my abilities to help her forget the ugliness of the day.

"It's getting harder to see." That part is true, but it doesn't explain the erection. My breath comes and goes in short pants. She can hear my desperation. She can sense the tension. The air is thick with it.

Worst of all, I know she sees it. She can't disguise her curiosity. It's as obvious as the boner between us.

While my eyes skim the water-logged streets, I watch her gaze drift back and forth from the road ahead to my lap. Every time it lands on my cock, she bites her lip then crosses and re-crosses her legs. She's unusually silent.

I don't pretend to know everything. But God's granted me certain gifts. I have a sixth sense about the stock market. I make one hell of a marinara. And I take seconds to detect a woman's arousal. Zelda's hot.

This is a recipe for disaster. I've got a lead pipe between my legs crying out for release and there's a beautiful doll eight inches away rubbing her thighs together for a cheap thrill. We're adults capable of fulfilling each other's needs.

And right now, I need Zelda.

8. ZELDA

Between the rain, the change in temperature and the humidity of our labored breaths, the fog clouding the windshield grows too thick for safety. Carlo's knuckles turn white as he grips the steering wheel and leans forward, squinting to see through the milky glass. It's impossible.

I crack my window and let a blast of cool air through. It gives us a brief glimpse of a parking lot two blocks ahead before our view disappears. But it's enough to set us on a course. I fall back into my seat and kick off my boots. By the look of the clouds ahead, we may be parked for a while.

Carlo squeezes my hand, lifting it to his lips as our eyes meet with a glimmer of expectation. I sink my teeth into my bottom lip and release a heavy sigh. My eyes make a southern inspection and verify he's still in business. *What business?* We're here as friends and we agreed no funny business would transpire, but he's clearly broken that rule by bringing that kind of weapon into the mix.

I tuck my legs underneath my behind and grind into my calves. No relief. None whatsoever. Everything I do makes things worse. I'm not losing my virginity in a car. I don't care if it's a Bugatti. But there must be other options available to a young woman in need. A handful come to mind, if only he'd make the first move.

Today's the day. I always said I'd wait until my wedding day and today *was* the day. I gave it my best try. *No more.* All my friends lost it years ago. I've been inundated with stories. Some good. Some bad. None nearly as sordid as the nastiness I had in mind for this very day.

And now it's here. I can't wait to meet someone new, date, work out my trust issues, fall in love, meet parents and plan another wedding. That could take years. I'm wilting. This flower needs watering. Why should I deny myself when there's a sexy Italian watering can a few inches away?

Carlo flips the turn signal and decelerates as we turn into an empty parking lot attached to the Cape Cod Visitor's Center. Everything's closed for the day or maybe the season, and I haven't seen another car in over ten minutes. We're alone. These tinted windows make it hard to see inside. Heavy rain conceals the rest.

He shifts the car to park. A beat passes. Sets the parking brake. Silence.

Screw propriety. I'll make the first move. My mind spins. Thoughts swirl a mile a minute. *If I swing my leg...No, wait a minute. If I lift my skirt, then swing my leg over his lap.* Shoot. Is there enough room?

Enough stalling. I'm going in. I close my eyes and take a deep breath to steel my nerves, but a sudden tug makes them fly open.

A firm hand clasps my waist and lifts me off my seat. Another hand travels up my thigh, grips my ass and I'm airborne. One counterclockwise twist later and I'm inches from Carlo's gorgeous face, straddling his muscular thighs. There's no time to react. No chance to speak.

We lunge.

Full lips fall on mine, and my hands land on his shoulders, holding him still, propping up my shuddering limbs as my body submits to nature. His tongue swipes mine and something sparks inside me. The scent of his sweat and taste of his breath ignite the flame. When his stiff cock lurches forward, bumping my swollen clit through my scandalously damp panties, I burst into a fiery blaze that burns away my useless inhibitions.

"What do we have here?" The deep tenor of his silvery voice vibrates into my chest, prickling my skin almost as much as the touch of his thick fingers creeping into my panties.

A pout forms. A childish whine falls from my lips. I lift my knees, tucking them under his arms, and grind forward. "I'm so wet. I need you to make it go away."

His warm hazel eyes grow wide. He runs his hand through my sodden mound and trails his fingers down my slit. Two fingers slide inside and his body tenses. His gaze returns to mine. With our lips a breath apart, he whispers and guides them inside me again. "How many men have had this pussy, Zelda?"

I shake my head, riding the forward motion of his broad fingers. "No one. I waited for today. But I can't wait anymore, Carlo. It's too hard. Let's go back to Boston." I pull my sweater over my head and toss it to the side. His mouth parts with surprise then falls open when I unhook my bra and push his face into my breasts.

"Jesus Christ, little girl." His mouth covers my nipple and the deep suckle combined with the penetrating force of his fingers hurls me into a sex-crazed frenzy that I'm convinced must have been lurking beneath the surface all along.

"Carlo! Take it out. Let me see it. Please, let me feel it against my pussy." My words stun him into a catatonic stupor, but his brain snaps back in seconds. He fumbles, unbuttons, unzips, digs into his pants then pulls out a hefty appendage that makes me gush with sincere admiration.

"Is this what you want?" He grabs both my thighs and tugs me forward. If he thinks I need encouragement, he's mistaken. I'm ready. I asked for this and I don't regret my words.

I nod and lift my skirt to my waist. "It's exactly what I want."

He clutches the nape of my neck and yanks me forward, sealing his lips to mine in a kiss that builds on a kiss that builds on another. My heart clamors in my chest, mistaking my lust for something grander. Butterflies crowd by belly, flapping their wings in jubilation, believing I've found my true love, but I swallow hard and suffocate them.

Love has nothing to do with this.

"You're so fucking beautiful. You take my breath away." His words slither into my heart before I have time to seal the borders. It's the sweetest thing anyone's ever said to me. *And the hottest.* Maybe Zara's right. Carlo has years of experience making women love him. I may be in over my head.

"Take what you want from me. I want to see you make yourself come on my cock." His smoldering gaze turns my brain to mush. I forget my concerns, wiggle closer and nudge my panties to one side. He helps me to my knees and watches me push his cock into my moist slit. The first drag strikes my clit and my knees buckle. He catches me by the arms and lifts my chin until our eyes meet in a fiery gaze that steels. With our eyes fixed and his hands left free to roam every curve of my trembling body, I grind into his heavy shaft.

"Carlo..." I've soaked his lap. My rhythm has a mind of its own. With every swipe, every bump and near miss into my inner depths, a tension building within tightens into a knot I can't seem to untie.

"Where do you want that cock, baby?" Carlo licks my

nipple, grazing his teeth against my sensitive skin and taunting the other with his fingers.

"Inside me!" My breath falters. I'm so close I can touch it. I just can't reach it.

"Are you sure you want me to break that little pussy? Do you think you can handle me? I won't go easy on you." He spanks my ass, light at first then harder. "Answer me, Zelda. Are you sure you can handle me?"

"Yes!" I inch closer to my reward.

"We're not going back to Boston." His fingers dive into my slit and punish my clit with such precision, I bounce and fall onto the steering wheel. Every stroke is a masterpiece. The knot I spent minutes tying unravels in seconds. Hazel eyes find mine and my body succumbs to a shattering fit of delicious bliss that propels me into another dimension. I'm stunned by his skill.

"We're not going back?" Panting and out of breath, I struggle to speak. More aware of my nudity, I use my hands to shield my breasts, but he nudges them away and uses his own to take their place.

Caressing my flesh, he shakes his head and trails kisses along my collarbone. "We'll stay in Chatham tonight. There's an inn by the shore with cottages. I've seen it before. We can stay there tonight. Your first time should be special. Are you sure this is what you want?"

His warm gaze sets my soul at ease. He's a good person. If I accept his limitations, he won't hurt me. I can live with that. I can only hope every man I love will be so forthcoming.

"It's what I want. And you don't have to worry, Carlo." I reach for my bra and guide it onto my shoulders.

His brow creases as he takes my hand and helps me back to my seat. "I'm not worried. Why would I worry?"

I shake out my sweater and raise it over my head, sliding it down through my arms. "You don't have to worry that I'll grow attached and want more. Just because I'm a virgin doesn't mean I don't understand your rules. I know this is one night. That's all I want too." I swallow the lump in my throat and offer a smile.

His expression hardens. "Of course. One night."

9. CARLO

THIS IS WHAT I WANT. *IT'S A WIN-WIN.* A HEART-STOPPING, VIRGIN temptress wants to have meaningless sex with me and then call it a day. If she hadn't spoken up, it would have forced me to reiterate my stance. She saved me the trouble.

It was a subject I desperately wanted to avoid. You can't introduce a woman to sex and then pull the rug out from under her after the fact. Although I've made my feelings known, I'd have an obligation to make sure she understood nothing had changed. Virginity isn't something I take lightly. It's been over twenty years since I've met a virgin in the wild. Innocence rarely attracts me. It comes with complications. And I abhor complications.

This is a good thing. I should be thrilled.

Then why haven't I said a word since we got back on the road?

As we approach the village, I loosen my grip on the steering wheel and roll my neck. Surely, my silence has given her second thoughts. Is that what I want? No, I might be annoyed but not displeased enough to surrender. She's piqued my interest more than I can describe. She's different. I can feel it. Something visceral commands me to seek her out. Years of experience urge me to run, and yet primal instinct demands I see this through.

The purpose escapes me.

She's right to set boundaries. It's best we limit ourselves to one night. I don't do relationships. I never have, and my fondness for Zelda Haverty won't rewire me. This is who I am.

"We're almost there." Strangled words emerge from my clenched throat in a voice I hardly recognize. Panic sets in. I could have blamed the awkward silence on my indifference or concern for the weather, but now she knows I'm angry. And if I'm angry, I care.

I wait a beat before I try to speak again. Maybe she'll say something first. She plays dumb. Not a peep from her side of the cabin. She doesn't move a muscle.

Is it horror? Is she horrified?

I take a deep breath and sigh, hoping to prompt a response. More silence. Rudeness, really. Perhaps Boston doesn't sound so bad after all.

Frustrated by her strange game, my scowl grows deeper. My jaw ticks. She may think I'm only good for sex, but she can still treat me like a human being. Fuming with rage, and ready to let her have it, I crane my neck to face her.

She's asleep. She must have fallen asleep as soon as we left the parking lot. The only awkward silence is mine. Zelda passed out in the afterglow of her orgasm. The orgasm I gave her.

My heart bursts with pride. My frown disappears. I've never been a humble lover. I aim to please and it feels good to have my work appreciated. Lost in self-praise, I don't hear her stir when we roll into the first stoplight.

"Are we there? Is this Chatham?" Her sleepy eyes flicker open and soft green irises pull me into their depths. My pulse quickens as visions of breasts, nipples, soft lips on mine and Zelda's writhing body on the cusp of ecstasy skitter through my brain.

Her tiny mouth stretches open in an adorable yawn and my heart flutters with infatuation. Then I imagine sliding my cock through those plump lips as far as she can take it, flipping her over, ripping off her panties and driving it home until she takes every last drop of come I have to give and screams for mercy.

Holy shit, where am I?

"Are you okay? The light's green." She quirks an eyebrow and points to the road.

I nod with zeal. "I'm good. Did you get enough sleep? Let's book a room before we head out to eat. I want to make sure we get something nice." I sound like a maniac, but she's so enthralled by the scenery she chooses not to mention it.

"Can we stop at a store to grab toiletries and extra clothes? There are a few things I'd like to pick up. You probably need condoms. Don't you?" She looks away shyly at the mention of condoms. Forty minutes ago, she begged to come on my cock, but now she blushes at the mention of condoms. It takes a bedroom, or something resembling it to bring out her naughty side. If we had more time together, that would be the first habit I'd break. I don't care how dirty we get. Our sex would always be sacred.

"We'll stop before we eat." I place my hand on her thigh and she scoots closer. One firm squeeze and she leans her head into my shoulder. We drive in silence, but there's nothing awkward about it. There's serene comfort in holding her close and I know she feels it too

We're two souls meeting in time. I think we've met before. Something tells me we'll meet again.

Zelda's my girl. *How will I walk away from my girl?*

10. ZELDA

"What's with the pearls?" Carlo unbuttons his shirt and watches me step out of the bathroom in the new teddy I purchased in town. My eyes fall to the thin coat of dark hair gracing his sculpted chest. The gray hair that dusts his head and beard hasn't reached the rest of his body. He's glorious.

I lift my hand to my collar and tighten the clasp. "I brought them in my purse. Do they look bad?"

He shakes his head. "Not at all. But I don't want to bust them in the heat of passion. Like I said, I'm not going easy on you." His stern tone pierces my heart. His exacting gaze melts me in a pool of sticky arousal. The knot in my belly returns, curling so tight, my thigh muscles clench and make it impossible to walk.

The last thing I want is easy. I want passion and fire. My sanity is at stake. I'd never survive Carlo making love to me. I'm too close to the edge as it is.

I take a deep breath, exhale slowly, and tiptoe a few more steps. Growing impatient, he drops his shirt and extends his hand to coax me over. A giggle bubbles up, but I quickly bite my lip to keep it from bursting free. This is no time for childish antics. He's a mature man. A beautiful mature man with an incredible body and an enormous erection waiting to make a woman out of me. *Oh God, that sounds ridiculous.* And a little hot, if I'm honest with myself.

"Zelda..." He steps closer and takes my hand.

My gaze falls to the deep horizontal lines rippling across his steely abdomen and my knees buckle. My mouth slacks. While my eyes flitter back and forth from his face to his abs, I stammer my strange reply. "I'll take them off if they get in the way. I have a fantasy about wearing them my first time."

His mouth curves into a sinister grin reminiscent of an old Hollywood villain. "You have a fantasy about wearing heirloom pearls? Why? I think I need to know why."

My eyes bug. In a hasty retreat, I step back and drop the straps on my teddy, revealing my breasts for his view. I shouldn't have said anything. It's ludicrous. Childish. If I can distract him, he'll drop it and get down to the business at hand.

His smile broadens, and his eyes gleam with naughty intent. He steps closer and fills his hands with both breasts. While caressing each mound with the care and admiration of a great aficionado, he leans into my shoulder and whispers, "You were saying."

"It's silly."

"Not to me."

"I fantasized about my wedding night. White lingerie. A honeymoon suite. Champagne. Then wearing nothing but my grandmother's pearls while I ride my husband dirty." Saying the words out loud makes it sound twice as bad as it did in my head. A quiet gasp escapes my lips. My eyes find his wide gaze. It must be curiosity. Carlo's been around the block. Something like that wouldn't sound dirty to a man like him. Would it?

"Dear God in heaven. That's the nastiest thing I've ever heard." His jaw falls open.

"Carlo!" Hot shame devours me. I stomp my foot and make a

run for the bathroom. I don't get far. Halfway there, a mix of hands and arms come together to propel me into the air and hurl me over Carlo's shoulder. When I put up a struggle, a hard smack on my ass yields my surrender.

"Quiet down, dirty girl. I'll let you keep your pearls on." He flips me over and tosses me onto the king-size bed. I bounce into the middle and readjust my straps. He doesn't get to stare at my tits while he teases me.

"No, it's ruined." I reach behind my neck and unfasten the clasp.

"Zelda Haverty! Not one more move." He unbuttons his pants and whips off his belt. I freeze, intrigued by his tone.

"Keep the pearls. You've given me a vision I'd like to see come to life. I may not be your husband, but I've got something you can ride dirty." He drops his pants, then slides his boxers down his legs. My hands drop. My shoulders sink. The air leaves my lungs.

"I couldn't possibly..." I swallow the saliva flooding my mouth then clutch my pearls. I'm not being modest. My fantasies didn't include an obstacle course.

He struts closer to the bed and my eyes focus on the hefty cock bobbing its way towards me. I rise to my knees and scamper forward to greet it. He catches me by the waist and folds me into his arms. "I think you can do anything you set your mind to, Zelda. And I want to see you try. Okay?" His lips fall on mine in sweet, tantalizing licks that tease me into seeking more. My lazy kiss deepens. Our tongues dance with desperation, entangling then foraging as he makes his way onto the bed.

"But no champagne, sweetheart. I don't want to deprive you of any sense. And I want you to remember every second of tonight. Because I will." He doesn't wait for me to answer. His warm eyes meet mine for no more than a second before he guides the lacy straps off my shoulders and easily slips the teddy off my trembling limbs.

"First, we live through one of my fantasies. Tasting this pussy. I've thought about this since you caught your bracelet on my button." My head shoots up with surprise then falls back, stunned when he spreads my thighs and drags his tongue through my slick folds. My gasps fall on deaf ears and my screams only egg him on. One punishing strike to my clit shatters me. A second alters my perception, sending mind-bending shock waves through all four limbs. My first orgasm comes like a freight train. No build up. No tension. Carlo pulls me into the deep blue sea of bliss like a tsunami of cataclysmic proportions.

"Carlo!" My voice breaks, as tears stream down my cheeks. I need a reprieve. A moment to catch my breath, but he doesn't let up.

"One more." His tongue flicks and swirls, striking my clit again and again until I lose my voice and resort to ceaseless whimpering, then sobbing. Nothing evokes mercy. He feasts like a savage animal until he feels my body tense. I cry out, shuddering on the verge of explosion, but his untiring devotion to my climax never wavers.

As pleasure peaks, my hips grind into his face, dousing his beard with my arousal. He doesn't care. He strokes harder, burying his tongue while his hands fumble with something I can't see.

He brutally drags it out. When the waves recede, he uses his fingers to bring back the tide, making me ride his hand while he strokes my clit into the start of a third climax.

I shamelessly surrender. As my head falls back, my legs fall open. Carlo growls under his breath and cups my pussy hard, drawing my tired eyes to his. "Is this little pussy ready to meet her new best friend?" He leans in and drags his cock, already sheathed in a condom, through my drenched slit.

I nod with enthusiasm. "Yeah." *Best friend?*

11. CARLO

 Why would I say something like that? At the most it's acquaintances, and if she has her way, we may never see one another again.

I thought I had this all figured out. What good are twenty years of experience if my carefully constructed wall of indifference can crumble in two days? The more time we share, the more this ache consumes me. I'm such a fucking joke.

I want to sexualize her. She wants me to treat this like a one-night stand. Objectifying her doesn't even feel disrespectful. But every time I try, I feel the noose tightening. It's not even a bad noose. It's a kinky noose that ends in mind-blowing orgasms for the rest of our lives.

If I knew how to love someone, I'd fall head over heels in love with her.

I can taste her sweet come on my lips. My heart races with memories of her virgin flesh on my mouth. Her honey still coats my throat, but I run my fingers through her folds and suck them clean to fill my mouth with her scent. The air is thick with her aroma. It's so heavy in my beard, I may not wash it out for days.

I'm ready to take her, but the dreamy look in her eyes slays me.

The curve of her breasts summons more than my average fantasy. It invites flashes of motherhood. Zelda bearing another man's babies. A vision my empty heart suddenly can't bear.

My heavy eyes sink to her voluptuous hips and the flat belly between them. I run my hand along her torso and imagine it growing, swollen with my seed. I can't think straight. This is lunacy. I should get dressed and get another room before I stay and rip this condom off my dick. I can't be trusted.

"Carlo?" Her arms reach out, her knees rise to meet my hips, and I forget everything but Zelda.

I crawl up, weave my fingers through her hands and stretch her arms over her head. With my knees, I guide her thighs to open wider, lifting them over my hips until she locks them around my back. My mouth molds to hers. Our lips taste and tease. With every kiss she returns, my passion for her grows until I need to break away or I fear I'll make an announcement I'll regret.

"Are you sure, baby?" I release her hands and feast on her amazing breasts, burying my face in her perfumed cleavage and suckling voraciously on the nipples of my dreams.

She runs her fingers through my hair, gripping tightly and encouraging my carnage. "Yes. I'm sure."

"Look at me. We're doing this now. This happens once in your life. I hardly remember my first time, but I don't want you to forget yours." I rut into her, slowly at first, dousing my cock in her entrance but never penetrating her more than a few inches.

She nods, panting, winding her legs higher on my back until we're in a perfect position. I breathe her in, whisper something against her skin only I can understand, and then fill her completely. She grips me tightly and clenches my shaft as she struggles to adjust. I pull out and a shuddering moan breaks free.

"Are you okay?" I kiss her pout and gauge her expression. She's so fucking beautiful. My heart slams into my sternum and breaks free from my ribs.

She nods and rolls her hips into mine. "Please, don't stop." She grinds into me again and my eyes roll back in my head. I plunge deep, stretching her open just for me. This is mine. I thrust again and again. *This is mine.* I'll figure this out. If I need to prove myself, I will. But I'll be damned if someone else gets a shot at my Zelda.

Jealousy ignites a flame that's never been lit. My blood boils with love and rage. I won't share this girl. Not this one. I don't care what I need to do. I'll lie. Steal. Stalk. Hound her incessantly until she lets me take her for a second date. But I'll make her mine.

Sometimes angry love is the best kind.

I unwrap her legs and lift her ankles to my shoulders, catching her by surprise. With one ass cheek in my hand, I thrust deep, ramming with fury and stroking her clit with such finesse, the overwhelming sensation of multiple orgasms barrels into her like a category five hurricane. Her hips jolt frenetically. Her hands reach for her tits, caressing and tugging her nipples in a wild display that brings tears to my eyes. I come so close to coming, I nearly forget about her dirty fantasy.

How could I forget?

"Time to ride Daddy dirty, princess." I clasp her waist and flip her over, straddling her on my hips until her pussy's centimeters from sliding down my cock.

"No, not Daddy." She pants, brushing her hair out of her face while she straightens her pearls. "That's what I call my fath..."

She loses her ability to speak as I ease her down onto my cock. Her lashes flutter wildly. Gasps flow freely. She sinks her pearly whites into her juicy bottom lip, adjusts her knees and breathes a guttural moan that nearly makes me come. "Oh, God, Carlo. I haven't made you come once. That's so selfish."

I hold her tits in my hands and bounce her on my lap. "That's what you think. I made myself come three times last night. Each time you were the only person on my mind."

Her eyes flare. She clutches her pearls and rides the rigid cock between her legs. Moaning freely. Lips quiver with every roll of her hips. Our eyes meet and it feels impossible to look away. Sweat drips down our faces, and something simmers between us that neither will say out loud.

I peek downward between us and see the space where our bodies join, where her tight pussy fights to swallow my cock. The sight sends me to the edge. I'm so close to crumbling, but she needs to come with me. That's all that matter tonight. We'll do this again. And we'll do it for real. I'll spill my seed inside her. Claim her the way I know I'm meant to claim every inch of her virgin body, but not tonight. I'll do it the right way.

I reach down and stroke her swollen clit, thumbing furiously until her body stiffens and she loses control. She flies forward and surrenders to my rhythm, riding me with such recklessness, she's too out of breath to speak. Her misty eyes hood. Her breasts heave as her back arches. While she bears down on my cock, trembling in a state of ecstasy, I catch sight of her grandmother's pearls still hanging proudly from her delicate neck. The sight leaves me speechless.

Such a filthy girl. Of course, she's mine.

12. ZELDA

THE SUN WAKES ME. IT FEELS DELIBERATE. WE TOOK ALL precautions. We drew the curtains and sealed the cracks. But a tiny one must have escaped us. Just before 7:00, a harsh beam of light lands directly on my eyes and frightens me out of my warm covers. But they don't feel as warm as they did last night. I stretch my arm underneath and feel for Carlo, then reach for his pillow.

"Carlo?" I sit up and look around the room. *Did he leave?* I know we said one night, but I thought he'd give me a ride home.

I swing my legs off the bed, stretch my back and pad into the bathroom. On my way, I see his wallet and Rolex watch sitting on the opposite nightstand. There's little doubt he left those behind.

I lift the heavy piece of metal and inhale the scent on the back of its case. It smells like his cologne. Cedar and bergamot with a hint of ginger. My brain floods with naughty endorphins. My mind spins with visions and memories I won't soon forget. Last night eclipsed my wildest expectations. It surpassed my fondest wish for my wedding night. Ethan would never have been such a considerate lover. It would have been over as soon as it began and if I didn't orgasm, he'd blame it on my biology, not his lack of skills or effort.

I'm such an idiot. I must have rushed into an engagement for want of sex. For want of love and a family. But I should have felt more for Ethan. At the very least, I should have felt this. What is this? This is different. I'm not sure how, but it feels bigger. More dangerous and yet somehow, safer. It doesn't make sense. And after today, it doesn't have to make sense. My torrid affair with my older man is over. Zara was right. They're good for what ails you.

I set his watch down and amble into the bathroom to start my shower. He must have gone for breakfast and taken a walk. This must be the part that gets awkward for him---the morning after.

Boo! The morning after! Marry me, Carlo!

I giggle to myself and run my hand through the stream to check the temperature. Carlo Novello doesn't need to worry his pretty head over me. I strut into the main bedroom and reach for my plastic bag of newly bought toiletries. I do hope he brings breakfast. We skipped dinner and surely burned over a thousand calories last night.

I step onto the tile and close the frosty door. The scorching water cascades like heavy rain over my sore muscles and soothes me into a state of bliss. The sound evokes fond memories. My nipples tighten with nasty thoughts. Sitting in Carlo's lap in a torrential downpour, riding his lap, rubbing his thick cock on my pussy until he made me come so easily it felt like he pressed a button inside me.

Fuck, why is it so easy for him? He's known me for two days and he knows my body better than me. It's not natural. It's not fair.

My belly tightens with that familiar ache. I run my hands over my tight peaks, caressing my breasts with foaming bath soap and remembering the feel of Carlo's masculine hands exploring every inch of my body. My skin prickles under the hot water as a rush of adrenaline sends tingles from my taut nipples into my clit.

I rinse off and will the sensation away. Carlo will be back and eager to return to Boston. This is no time to indulge in self-love. Stepping wide, I grab the hand shower and allow water to pass between my thighs. The power spray strikes my swollen bud and sends me reeling into the shower wall.

What the shit?

I try it again, and my knees buckle, sending me to the floor. It must be a fluke. I've had a hand shower for years. Why hasn't anyone ever mentioned this fascinating feature? I crawl to the opposite side of the shower, lean into the wall and work my way into a standing position. After a quick adjustment, a better angle and a fast drink of water to relieve my thirst, I let her rip.

One orgasm follows another until my trembling legs turn to jello. There's so much steam, I can't see. The water's so loud, I never hear Carlo's footsteps.

Arms surround me and lift me seamlessly off the tile. Lips seize mine. Desperate, wordless kisses overwhelm me and leave me breathless. He leans me into the shower wall and my legs fit perfectly around his hips. This feels like something out of a movie. A hot older man surprises me in the shower while I'm getting ready for school and... *Oh, my God!* His thickness impales me, filling me to the hilt in one brutal thrust. I scream, then tighten my grip, riding him hard as the perfect orgasm sends me spiraling into lunacy.

"Who said you could come without me?" Carlo's animal grunts bounce off the walls. His fingers dig into my ass as he plows into my slick pussy, battering it, laying claim to every space inside me.

"Where...where...were you?" I whimper and claw his back, as the wet friction renders me a babbling idiot.

"I went for a walk." His dark gaze meets mine and his thrusts slow. Something's wrong. *Is that anger? Pain?*

A sudden realization hits. Panic strikes and I slide down his legs. In my lusty haze, I'd forgotten about condoms. "Carlo, I told you I'm not on the pill. You didn't finish, did you?" I rush out, swipe my towel off the rack and rush into the bedroom to check.

He follows me. "I didn't come, Zelda. I wouldn't do that to you. Why were you masturbating in the shower? Didn't you get enough last night?" He brings me into his lap and towels me off, using another towel to pad my hair. When he's done, I wipe his face and notice a hint of red in his eyes. *Was it the shower?*

I lean into his chest and make light of an awkward situation. He can't be that hurt. We're not in a relationship. And even if we were, it's hardly considered cheating. *Right?* I'm not familiar with these types of details. "Does that hurt your feelings? It was an accident. I discovered the shower head nozzle works wonders."

"Are you ready to go?" He kisses my shoulder and sighs. Maybe he'll miss me. I'll miss him too. I'm happy a piece of me got under his skin. Carlo Novello is who he is and I'm glad I got to know him better. He's not as bad as they say. He's not bad at all.

"Give me twenty minutes, I'll buy us breakfast."

13. CARLO

"He's had something stuck up his ass all week. He's driving everyone crazy. I cancelled the rest of his appointments after he gave one of his best clients horrible investment advice on Monday. Cost the guy a small fortune and then he had the balls to say it was his fault for gambling on the stock market." June and Susan stand side by side at my door, the door I specifically closed twenty minutes ago, and talk about me like I'm not standing fifteen feet away.

"Did you call his mother?" Sue laughs at my expense, hoping she'll piss me off enough to make me talk. No one knows about Chatham. I haven't spoken about Zelda to them or anyone else. There's no sense in beating a dead horse.

We went our separate ways on Sunday and haven't spoken since later that night. She got what she wanted. I served my menial purpose in her life, and now I can go back to doing what I do best. Meaningless sex with women I don't love.

What could be more satisfying than that?

My breath hitches. The burning ache in my heart expands and threatens to devour me whole. I turn away from my laptop and duck behind the safety of my larger monitor. Although tears obscure my vision, I sense June creeping closer.

"Jesus Christ! Is he crying again? Goddamn it, Sue. You went too far! I invited you here to get him to talk and all you do is drive the knife into his heart." June marches towards my desk with a handful of tissues.

"I just asked if you called his mother. That was an honest question. I'm sorry, Car..." Sue stammers and fights to get through the door before June slams it in her face.

Treading lightly, she wrings her hands and approaches with a remorseful tone. I take her tissues and wipe my eyes. I feel ridiculous, but I don't have the strength to hide my tears. "Hey big guy, did something happen with your mom?"

I make the connection. No wonder she sent Susan away. Why else would I cry? It couldn't possibly be over a woman. Carlo Novello doesn't know how to love. I brought this on myself. I've shunned love all my life. It never suited me. It was inconvenient and boring.

Then God sends me a miraculous creature to bring me to my knees. I get a taste of what I've missed. But only a taste. Just enough to torment me the rest of my days. No one to cherish or warm my bed. That honor's reserved for better men than me.

"Carlo! For heaven's sake! You're scaring me. Are you broke? Is your mom sick? Did someone steal your identity? Did you knock someone up? Holy shit! You're impotent!" She falls into the chair in front of my desk and covers her gaping mouth.

My heart stops. Tears cease and my sadness turns to horror. "Impotent? Are you trying to give me a heart attack?" I point to the edge of the desk closest to her. "Knock on wood. Now, June."

She knocks once. When I quirk an eyebrow, she knocks again. "Happy?"

I nod and fold my arms at my chest. "This has nothing to do

with my mother. For your information, I'm...heart..." The rest of the word stays lodged in my throat. "Heart..." My eyes mist. I've never said it out loud. "Heartbr... I don't want to talk about it."

Her expression softens. Her lip quivers, but she bites down to hold in her pout. "Carlo..." She covers her heart. "Who broke your heart?"

I lean my elbows into my desk and bury my face in my hands. "You'll just make fun of me. And I know I deserve it. I'm going to die alone, June. You were right. I'm an old futon. No one wants me."

She sucks in a breath and skitters around my desk. In a rare and uncomfortable move, she throws her arms around my shoulders and gives me a hug. "Fuck! Don't cry! I'm sorry I called you a futon. I promise I didn't mean it. Your mother put me up to it. She said it was the only way to get you to stop being such a whore. She wants grandchildren."

"What?" I squirm away to get a handle on this new information. "My mother told you to hurt my feelings?"

She nods and slinks back to her side of the desk. "You're her only son. Her only child. She's growing desperate. But that has nothing to do with your heartbreak. You don't deserve to die alone, Carlo. You're not a bad guy. That's why women love you so much. You make them feel beautiful. Who broke your heart? Maybe I can help."

I pull my phone out of my coat pocket and scroll to Zelda's outdated Instagram. Her last post was six months ago, the day she received her grandmother's pearls. I've saved that photo and memorized each pearl on that necklace. She's so fucking adorable. I can't believe she thought wearing her grandmother's pearls was akin to pornography.

"What's that?" June breaks my concentration.

I scroll to my favorite photo and slide the phone to June. It's a silly shot of her wearing red pajamas and a goofy smile last

Christmas morning. She looks sleepy and dazed, just the way she did after I nailed her four times Saturday night. That's such a good look on her.

"Zelda Haverty? Seriously? She's darling. She wouldn't hurt a fly. What did you do?" She scrolls through my phone without my permission and drops it when she sees something incriminating.

"You slept with her?" She jumps out of her chair and holds her hands at her waist. "You know she's vulnerable. What happened? Was she a virgin? Oh, my word, Carlo Novello! Did you deflower Zelda Haverty? You're twice her age!"

I reach for my phone and see my Sunday morning photo of half-naked sleeping Zelda. My second favorite photo. "We spent time together and had sex. We agreed to one night early on, but the more time I spent with her, the more I changed my mind. I didn't want one night. I wanted her. Saturday night, I came close to telling her, but I chickened out. Then, Sunday morning, I called my shrink at the crack of dawn and he convinced me to wait before I confess my feelings. He thought my interest stemmed from wanting what I couldn't have. I'd just blow it the way I blow everything else."

"Your shrink!" She paces and bites her nails. "That quack makes so much money off your misery. He doesn't want you to be happy. I told you to fire him."

I shake my head. "He has a point. Zelda's vulnerable and I need to get it right. I asked her to dinner when we got home, but she shut me down. She said we shouldn't invest any more time with one another. When I told her I thought it was worth a try, she looked me in the eye and said it wasn't."

June's eyes fill with tears. "You're so smart in business. When did you become such an idiot in life?"

"What?"

"Oh look, today's Zelda's twenty-second birthday." She scrolls through her phone and pulls up a photo of Zelda wearing a black string bikini strutting her hot ass down a beach in Cozumel.

I snatch the phone out of her hands and zoom in. It's Zelda's sister's account. My heart sinks. A group of men hover nearby, licking their chops while they stare at my Zelda's firm round ass with evil intentions. I click out into the feed then look at photo after photo of Zelda in different bikinis, each one smaller than the next. They're all obscene. Whatever happened to one piece bathing suits? Isn't Mexico a Catholic country?

Was this the sexual tour she had in mind?

My pulse skyrockets. My hackles rise and a rumbling growl stirs within. *No fucking way.*

What the hell am I doing here? This isn't like me.

I kick my legs and fly out of my chair. "I guess this is why she didn't want me. Why get tied down to an old futon when there are tons of swarthy young men to enjoy?" Seething with righteous indignation, I reach for my coat and storm out of my office.

June sprints passed me, babbling nonsense I'm too angry to hear. When the elevator door opens, she spreads her arms and blocks my entrance. "Hold up, cowboy. I called you a futon. Not her. You don't get to be angry at her."

I start to correct her, but she holds out her palm. "No! You don't get to be angry at her! You half-assed your declaration of love. I know you and you don't half- ass anything, Carlo. You were terrified the first woman you've ever loved would reject you, and you made a soft sale. Women don't wait almost twenty-two years and screw the first random man that comes along. She chose you and kept the rules I'm sure you set from the start. Just because you don't deserve her doesn't mean she doesn't love you. Maybe she likes futons."

"Stop calling me that." My broken heart shatters.

"Fine, I'll stop. But if you wanted her, you wouldn't have asked her to dinner. You wouldn't have asked her to give it a try. That's for pussies. And you're not a pussy." She taps the down button and slides out of the way.

She's right. I told myself I'd fight for her and then folded like a cheap suit. I'm not a pussy. I'm Carlo Novello. And I love Zelda Haverty. *Zelda Haverty Novello.* I like the sound of that.

Goddamn, that girl's in so much trouble parading around a foreign country in nothing but dental floss... Nope. No sense getting pissed now. I'll save it for her ass.

I step into the elevator and turn to face June. "I won't be in on Monday. I'm going to Mexico."

14. ZELDA

"Sweetie, eat something. You've hardly had a bite all week. Your bikini tops are fitting a tad loose." She's not wrong. It's always the first place I lose weight. Zara generously butters a roll and places it on a napkin besides me. She knows carbs are my greatest weakness.

I take a nibble and choke on it. My throat's too clogged with sadness to let anything through. I take a sip of water and try again. Zara worries and I haven't been forthcoming with information. She only knows it's about Carlo.

"Would you like to hear my Conall story? I've been saving it for a rainy day." She scoots her chair closer and tries to shake some life into my sagging limbs.

"It's okay. If you loved him, don't tell me. You shouldn't share something that meant so much to you." I cover my mouth to hide my pout, but it's no use. My dewy eyes give me away.

Zara's pale face turns bright red as her features twist into a heavy scowl. "Zelda Rosalind Haverty, I won't tolerate your tight lips one more second. What the hell happened? Did he turn you down? Did you have sex? Are you in love with Carlo Novello? Talk to me. I'm your big sister. God put me on this earth to help you and you've handicapped me all week!" She whips up some fake tears to make me talk.

"Stop making this about you." I push away from the table and head back towards the room.

She wouldn't dare dream of dropping it. Hot on my heels, she slams into my back and pushes me into the elevator. "Did you lose your V-card?"

I shriek and swat her with my purse. "I hate that expression. If you must know. Yes, I gave him my flower." I hold my head up and press the button to the sixth floor.

"Ew! You talk like Nana!" She shakes off the willies and pushes me into the wall. "And how was it? Was he as good as they say?"

My face catches fire. My fists clench at my sides. Jealous rage spears my heart. "Who says what?! What are you talking about?"

She shrugs and steps out with the bell, having effectively blown my mind. "I don't know. People say Carlo's a great lover. He's got a rep. Sorry. But you knew this."

I storm past her with my key card ready. "This is why I can't talk to you."

She catches my arm and swings me into a small patio overlooking the ocean. Walking ahead, she points to an outdoor sofa surrounded by tall lanterns. "Sit. Now. I'm not asking for raunchy details. Tell me what went wrong."

I shift my eyes from side to side, hug my chest, and drag my tired body onto the couch. The smell of the ocean breeze reminds me of Chatham. Everything reminds me of Chatham. Mexico looks nothing like Massachusetts, but I see Carlo everywhere. While Zara looks on, I bring my elbows to my knees and bury my face in my hands. And just like nothing, my heart explodes. Heavy sobs come so fast, I don't know I'm crying until I hear primal wails emerge from somewhere deep in my soul.

"I let him in." I stammer, stupefied by the ache in my heart. "I promised I wouldn't. I didn't think I had, and he crept in when I wasn't paying attention. He made love to me. He wasn't supposed to make love to me. I think he tricked me into loving him, Zara!" I stand up and hold my finger in the air, certain I've cracked some giant mystery.

She runs to my side and leads me back to the couch. "How did it end? Did he say thanks for the ass, and I'll catch you later? What happened? You agreed to one night. Is that what he wanted too? Maybe he wanted more." Zara tries to make excuses for him, but I won't have it. She doesn't know what I know.

"He acted weird and then asked me to dinner. He said maybe we should try to make something happen. *Maybe we should try?* I might not have much experience, but I know what that means. He'll just drag me deeper into his world. After I'm hooked, he'll remember he doesn't do relationships. By that time, I'll never get over him. Look at me! One night and I'm a wreck. Can you imagine what a week or a month might do?" I lift the hem of my dress and dab my tears.

"Cut him some slack. That's a big move for someone like him. That might be the biggest move he's ever made. Do you love him?" She kneels in front of me and takes my hand. "Well, do you?"

I shake my head and growl. "It doesn't matter. I'll get over him the same way I got over Ethan. A leopard doesn't change his spots. Carlo is who he is, and he'll never change." I lift the hem of my billowy cotton dress and march towards the room. I'm only a few steps away when I hear the sound of Zara's laughter.

I skid in my flip-flops and whip my head to give her the stink eye. "What the hell's so funny about your sister's heartbreak?"

"You better hope a leopard can change its spots, or that means *you'll* never change. That means you'll always be the girl who's too oblivious to see her fiancé didn't love her. And don't kid yourself. You're over him because you didn't love him either. Carlo won't be so easy, little sister." She smirks as she skitters past me towards the room.

I gasp dramatically and scamper away from the door.

"Where are you going?" Zara screams.

"To the beach. Maybe I'll walk right into the ocean and drown myself!" I sway my arms with the full force of someone trying to make a point.

"Fine. I'll call the coast guard in the morning. Love you."

15. CARLO

ON THE BEACH? THAT COULD BE ANYWHERE.

I throw my jacket into the corner of the room, rip off my shirt, tear off my pants and jump into a pair of swim trunks. I don't care about getting dirty, but I want to be ready to chase her into the water if that's where I need to go. She's not getting away. Not this time.

Zara's directions were vague, but her enthusiasm gave me hope. Maybe Zelda loves me. If she doesn't, I'll earn it. I'll win her heart because it's mine to win.

With the sun setting over the water, I walk onto my balcony and scan the sand for a woman in a white dress. A couple prances into view, canoodling while they walk and filling my heart with dread. I rush into my suitcase and grab my binoculars. It's not her. Thank goodness, there won't be a need to commit murder.

I look farther down the strip, past a pair of lonely palm trees with a hammock stretched between them. Sitting nearby, a few feet from the water, I make out a white dress and waves of dark hair blowing in the wind. *Bingo*. It's my girl.

There's no time to waste. Zelda's waiting. I skid across the marble floor and swipe my keycard off the dresser.

I spritz on cologne. Did I forget anything? My gaze falls on the box of condoms sitting pretty in my luggage. I eye them with disgust. *Never again.* I'm taking my lady bare. I'm closing this fucking deal once and for all, and if I need to get her dirty, so be it.

Besides, my mother's been patient long enough. Maybe we can give her a grandbaby before next Christmas.

She doesn't hear me coming. The sound of the ocean and the soft sand under my feet mutes my footfalls, allowing me to come close enough to smell her perfume. I've practiced everything I need to say a hundred times on my way here, but the tears streaming down her mottled cheeks send me into a whirlwind of doubt and panic.

"I have no right to ask for your love." Strange words I haven't rehearsed spring forth.

With a tiny jump, she cranes her neck, and those mossy green eyes lock on mine. A choir of angels sing in my head. My pride dies a fiery death. Every ounce of ego sinks into the sand as I fall to my knees in front of the only woman I've ever loved. "Zelda Haverty, you're magic. You mystified me the moment you first looked into my eyes. I love you. I love you. I love you. I don't want to try to be with you. *I need to be with you.* And we'll work because we're meant to work. Because I'll die if we don't work. I'll die without you."

"Carlo..." She covers her quivering lip and wipes a never-ending stream of tears. "But... but you said you don't do relationships. You said..." She hiccups and shields her face.

I take her hand and lift her into my lap, straddling her over my hips. "But I'll do this one. I'll marry Zelda Haverty, and that's the only relationship I'll ever need. I've never loved anyone but you, sweetheart. Can you love me, baby?" I lean my forehead into hers and breathe in the scent that's haunted me for days.

"I love you." She brings her sweet lips to mine and kisses away five days of soul-wrenching pain. "I loved you from the start. But we don't have to talk about marriage right away, we have all the..."

I interrupt her nonsense. "No, we don't."

"We don't?"

I reach under her dress, pull her panties to one side and smile when my fingers sink into the warmest honey. "I saw those photos, baby. How dare you show all of Mexico what belongs to me. You must be out of your mind." I flick her hard button and she jolts straight into my stiff cock. While she defends herself, I fumble it out of my shorts.

"Not ALL of Mexico. This place is inclusive. And it's practically empty." Her sorry excuse begs for a spanking. And she gets one.

I clasp her thighs and help her climb onto my cock. She shudders to adjust to every inch but works me in, grinding down to build a rhythm. True to form, I don't go easy. I work her hard, thrusting with avarice until she can hardly keep up with the ruthless pace I set.

"Slower, baby?" I don't mean a word. My blood's on fire.

"No! Faster!" She stuns me with her lust.

My heart thumps out of my chest. Her breath catches with every brutal thrust. Our lips crash with one fiery kiss after another. I can't get enough of my angel. She rides me harder, meeting every thrust, bouncing wildly until she gasps and throws her arms around my neck. Her thighs clench. Her tight pussy swallows my shaft in quick pulses that make my eyes roll back in my head.

"Carlo! I missed you..." Her soft voice breaks me. Love consumes me. I hold her wrists and toss her backwards into the sand.

"You'll never miss me again, sweetheart. I'm here. I'm yours." I plunge deep and reckless. She lifts her legs and wraps them around my waist.

"I want to be your husband. Will you have me?"

"Yes!" Her toes curl, but she repeats herself just in case I misunderstood her *yes*. "I'll have you. I love you."

"I love you, Zelda." I hold her gaze and the world stops around us. Only we exist. On this beach. Making love and promising to spend the rest of our lives together.

She cries out, lifts her hips, and pulls me in and out, shattering in a pool of soggy bliss. Her flesh clenches around me and I hold her tight as sticky warmth spreads between us. I fill every space and savor every moment of sealing her fate to mine. It's everything. I'm hers and I've wanted nothing more than this.

When she curls into my arms, I don't feel like a futon anymore. I'm the sweetest couch in the showroom. The one she takes home.

"I'm yours, Carlo." She gushes and kisses my chest.

"I know. You don't have a choice, sweetheart."

"Tell me something. The first time we had sex... or made love."

I correct her. "We made love."

"You mumbled something. I don't think you meant for me to hear you, but I've racked my brain trying to figure it out." She's so clever. Nothing slips past her.

With a smile on my face, I kiss the top of her head and think back to Saturday night. "No, I think I wanted you to hear it. I told you I loved you."

16. EPILOGUE- THREE YEARS LATER

ZELDA

I didn't read about it because I hate those society rags but according to my friend Evie, the Wells family were stunned when they heard that their precious boy's former fiancée, Miss Zelda Haverty married billionaire financier, Carlo Novello three short weeks after the cancellation of her original wedding. But that's not the worst of it.

To add insult to injury, their firstborn baby made her hazel-eyed debut at Massachusetts General Hospital less than nine months after the blessed event. Can you believe that?

Can you believe the nerve?

Mother thought we should have waited. Daddy said absolutely not. He holds grudges, and if my wedding made Ethan look bad, he was happy to take out a page announcing it in the Boston Globe. And Nana agreed.

This was before anyone knew Carlo knocked me up. When that part came out, everyone jumped on board.

We were thrilled. And now that he's provided a granddaughter with another on the way, Carlo's mother lives on cloud nine.

I pad into the nursery to check on Gabrielle, tiptoe past Carlo asleep in a rocking chair and stroll back to get ready for my commencements. I graduate from college today. My last year took forever to complete. It's entirely my fault. I took time off for my first wedding, then time off for the pregnancy and baby, but I finally wrapped things up this year.

I lay out my dress and grab Nana's pearls. I promised her I'd wear them today. After I look in on Gabs one more time, I head for the shower.

I'm excited to see Evie. She left Boston shortly before my wedding. *Talk about scandals.* She was right all along. She always said her family was out to get her and they definitely got her. Fortunately, things worked out better than she ever imagined. She married the king of her hometown and became its bonafide queen. I kid you not. But she doesn't care about those things. She's crazy about him.

He's a lot like Carlo. *There's just something about older men.*

I step into the shower, toss my towel and turn on the water.

"What are you doing?!" Carlo's stern voice almost makes me slip.

"Sweet Jesus! I'm pregnant and you're going to give me a concussion." I grab the hand shower and spray water on him.

He wipes his face and pulls off his shirt. His eyes narrow. He unzips his jeans, slides them down with his boxers and kicks both to the tile. "I'm on to you, Mrs. Novello. You did a double check on Gabby and me. You wanted to make sure I was asleep. But I was faking." He points, grabs the nozzle and splashes my breasts.

"I did not. There's no time for that. I need to get ready." I lather up my arms and use the hand shower to wet him down. "We have a long day with family and friends. We don't need to do anything tonight. Just tell me you're proud of me."

He nods. "Always. You're magnificent in all things. I always said you can do anything you set your mind on. You better believe I meant it."

I hand him a bottle of shampoo and he massages a dollop into my hair. While he works it in, he rubs my "best friend", *big Carlo*, into the small of my back and taunts me with a quickie. "I asked my mother to babysit tonight after graduation. I'm taking my girl to Monty's."

I hum and lean into his stiff cock. "You are?"

"Yep. I'm buying my college grad a virgin Cape Cod, maybe two, then taking her for a nice dinner to celebrate."

"I'm listening." I reach around my back and grip his shaft.

"And when we come home, I think I'll strip my nasty girl down to her pearls and make her ride her husband dirty."

The memory heats my cheeks and makes me laugh out loud. I sweep around to face him then hop into his arms. "You are such a dirty old man."

"Baby, I will always be *your* dirty old man."

THANKS FOR READING!

ABOUT THE AUTHOR

Lover of words, dachshunds, books, travel and anything with Nutella.

I write short stories, Steamy, Erotic Romance & Romantic Erotica . Don't look for slow burn or sweet & clean romances here.

If you're looking for a lot more content, check out my main pen name, Matilda Martel

My stories are about smart, sexy women & the alpha men who adore them.

InstaLove & InstaLust in the past, present & future -Sigh.

These are all quick reads-- romantic, dirty, sometimes a bit sleazy, but always with a HEA for our heroine.

For a free ebook, sign up for my Newsletter.

ALSO BY MATILDA MARTEL

DO YOU LOVE STEAMY AGE GAP ROMANCE?

Those are my favorites.

If you like them as much as me,

you might like these titles:

My Second Chance

Takeover

Blindsided

Get Your Kicks

The Pastor

In Praise of Older Men

My Heart's Desire

Maestro

Gilded Cage

Love Match

Play Right

The Man I Love

Bad Boss

Clever Girl

Chasing Zoe

The Good Girl

My Ward

Do you love Billionaire Romances?

Try these titles:

Takeover

Filthy Rich

Filthy Love

Blindsided

Magic Man

Hostile Takeover

There She Goes

Agreeably Arranged

Bad Boy

Do you love Friends to Lovers?

Shut Up & Kiss Me

Unsuitable

Lucky Man

Marry Me

Do you love Mafia Romances?

Check out my BROOKLYN BAD BOYS

Love Interrupted

Love Unleashed

Love Revealed

BAD BOYS TURNED GOOD?

Check out SCOUNDRELS IN LOVE

Bad Professor

Bad Boss

Bad Boy

PHILLY BOYS FIND LOVE IN LOVE BITES

Love Hate

Love Nest

Love Match

And many more!

Thanks for reading and I hope you come back again!